Kayli [signature] #7

Tuck the Puck

By Kaylie Globke

TREE NOOK HOUSE

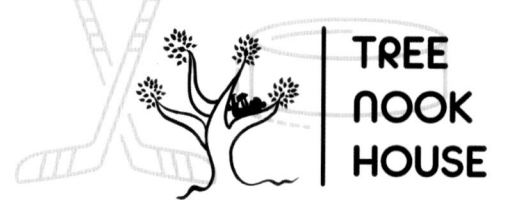

Tuck the Puck by Kaylie Globke.
Published by Tree Nook House LLC.
www.treenookhouse.com

No part of this publication may be reproduced in whole or in part, or stored in a retrieval system, or transmitted in any form or by any means, electronic mechanical, photocopying, recording, or otherwise, without written permission of the Publisher/Author.

For information regarding permission, write to www.treenookhouse.com.

Text & llustration Copyright ©2025 by Kaylie Globke

Illustrations by Valeshka Escalona

ISBN 979-8-9928036-0-0 (hardcover)

I dedicate *Tuck the Puck* to my husband, Al, and our children. I love how God brought us together through our favorite sport, hockey. My world is colorful and vibrant because of you. Being a wife and mamabear is truly my greatest achievement. I love you all so much. I hope this book serves as a cherished family heirloom that is passed on through our family generations.

Tuck the Puck is made from rubber with round edges to glide fast wherever he goes.

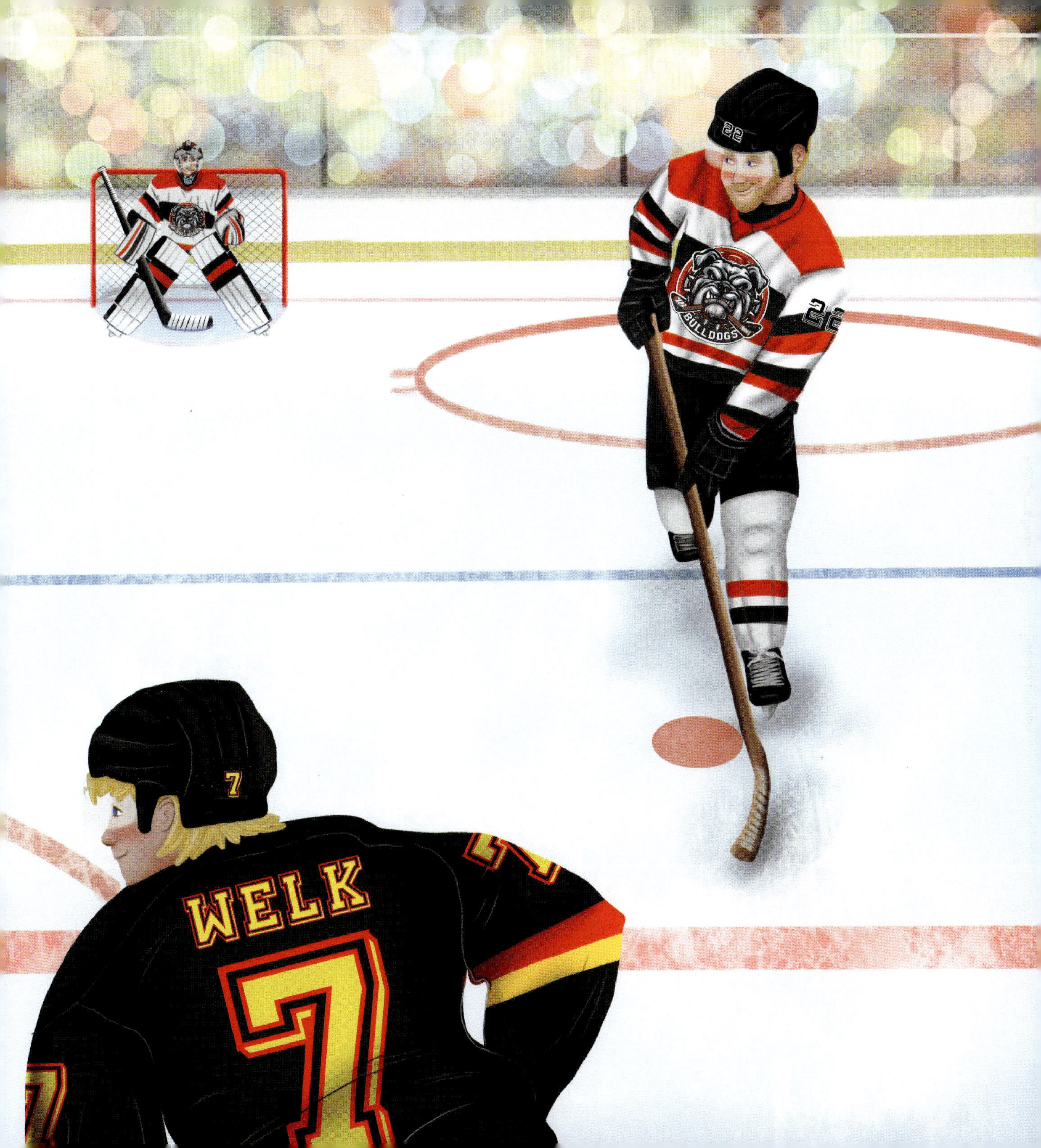
WELK
7

Tuck is repeatedly shot with a hockey stick at nets and clothing dryers to practice keeping goalies on their toes.

You miss **100%** of the shots you **don't** take
- *Wayne Gretzky*

Tuck finds himself traveling in hockey bags . . .

. . . buses and . . .

. . . even planes too.

When he arrives at his destination, Tuck is stacked with other pucks on the bench . . .

. . . before hockey players warm up for their game as you hear the crowd chant, "WOOHOO!"

The referee skates by super fast.

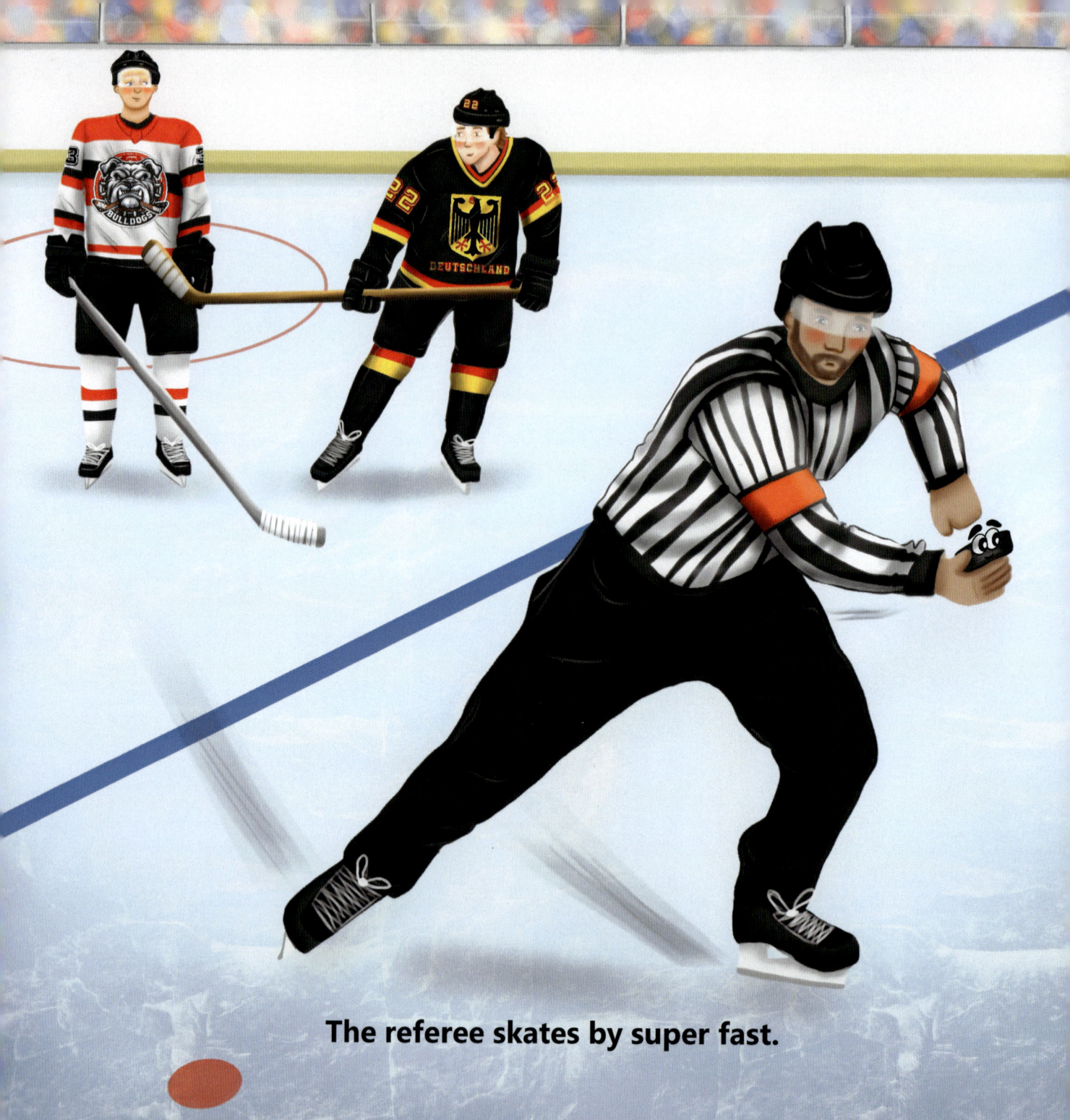

He picks up Tuck to drop at center ice as the players battle to win the draw, SLASH! SLASH!

Tuck dangles through players, SLAP! SLAP! TICK! TICK! **Passed from player to player, he is ever so quick.**

Seeing Tuck in action, the crowd lets out a "ROARRRRR!"
No one can stop him now – look at him soar.

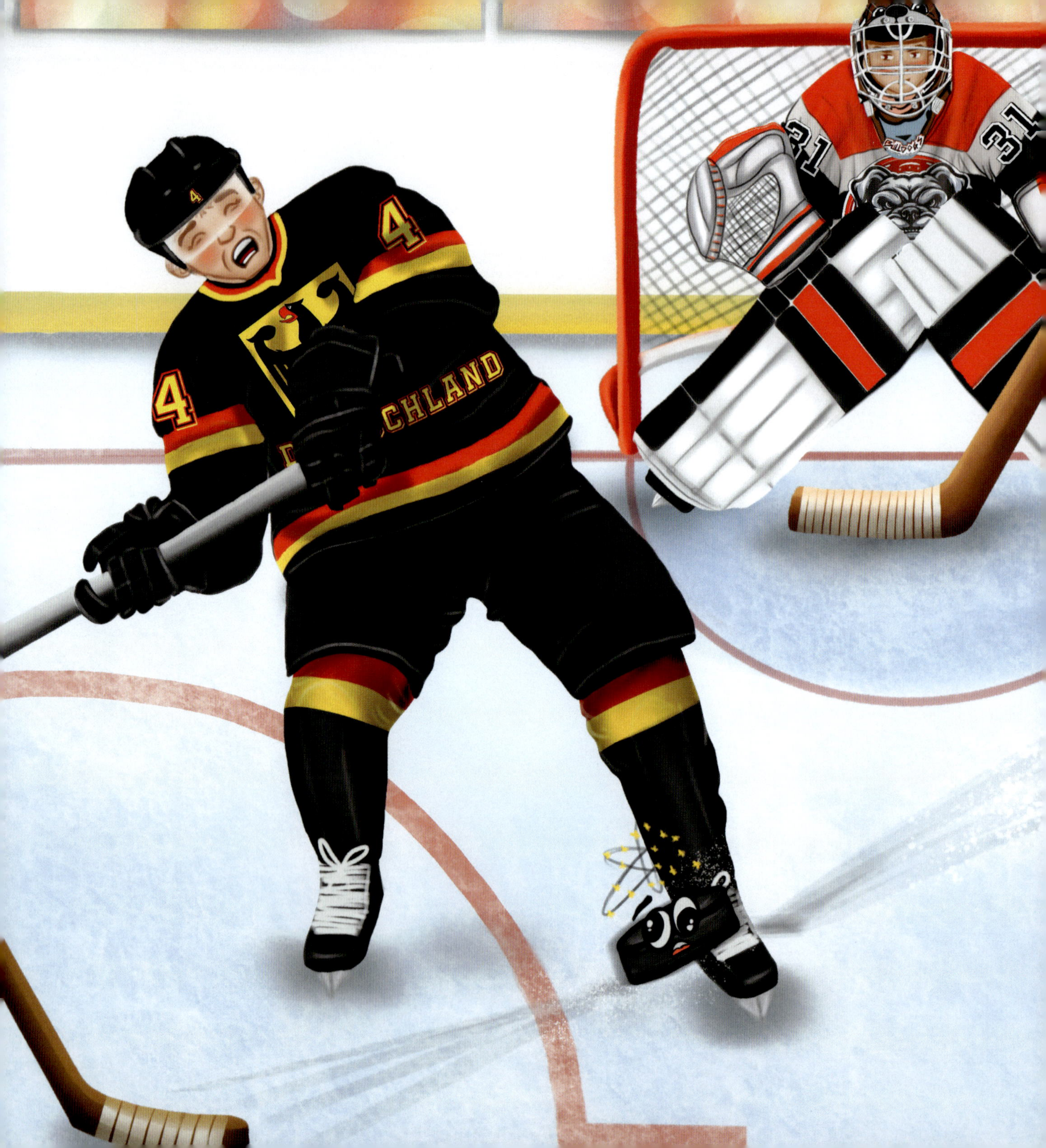
4
31

Hockey fans watch Tuck slide all over the place. He hits the boards, the sticks, and once in a while, a players' skate and lace,

"OUCHHHHH!"

Tuck flies through the air, but can still hit the goalie's post with the sound of a TINK!

He may even leave a dent or black scuff on the post as a reminder that he's small, but mightier than you may think.

Tuck scores goals that lead to victories, creating memories that last a lifetime.

He is handed to players after the game to keep for first goals and hat tricks where in the locker room, "WE WON, WE DID IT!" the players chime.

Famous NHL hockey players love Tuck so much they even share him with their fans. They throw him over the glass, PLUNK, so boys and girls can catch him in their hands.

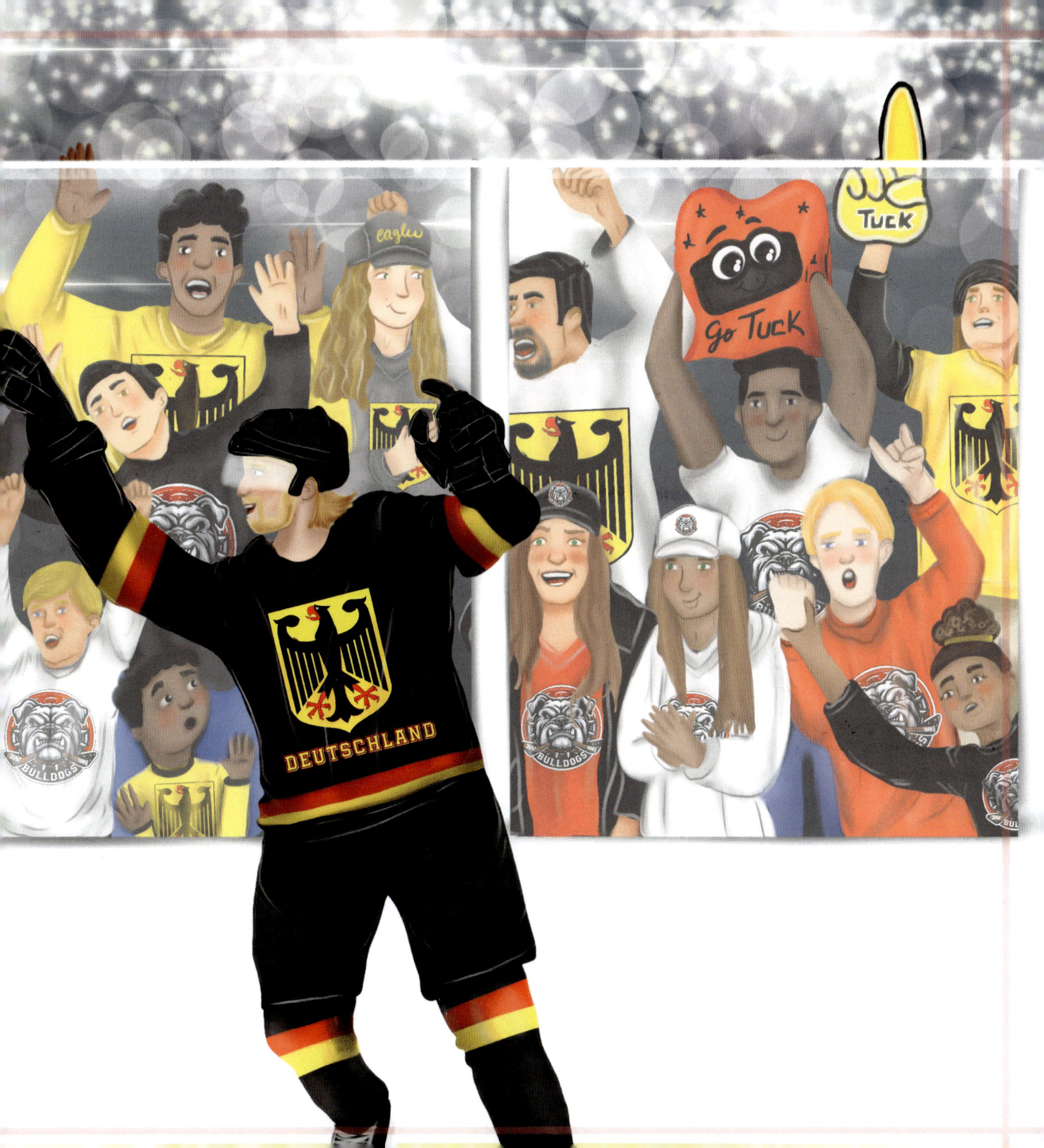
eagles
TUCK
Go TUCK
DEUTSCHLAND
BULLDOGS
BULLDOGS

Tuck is used in practice for more than games and goals too.

He is stick handled, spun around cones and caught in a glove.

He's flipped in the air, bounced on a stick blade and passed between players.

He is definitely loved.

He visits indoor and outdoor rinks where children laugh and play.

Tuck also visits the NHL Stanley Cup finals and Olympic gold medal games still to this day. NO WAY?!

Tuck travels from city to city, coast to coast and nation to nation, bringing the great game of hockey to all corners of the earth.

Sometimes Tuck isn't even played with on the ice. Sometimes he's on the ground, cement or turf.

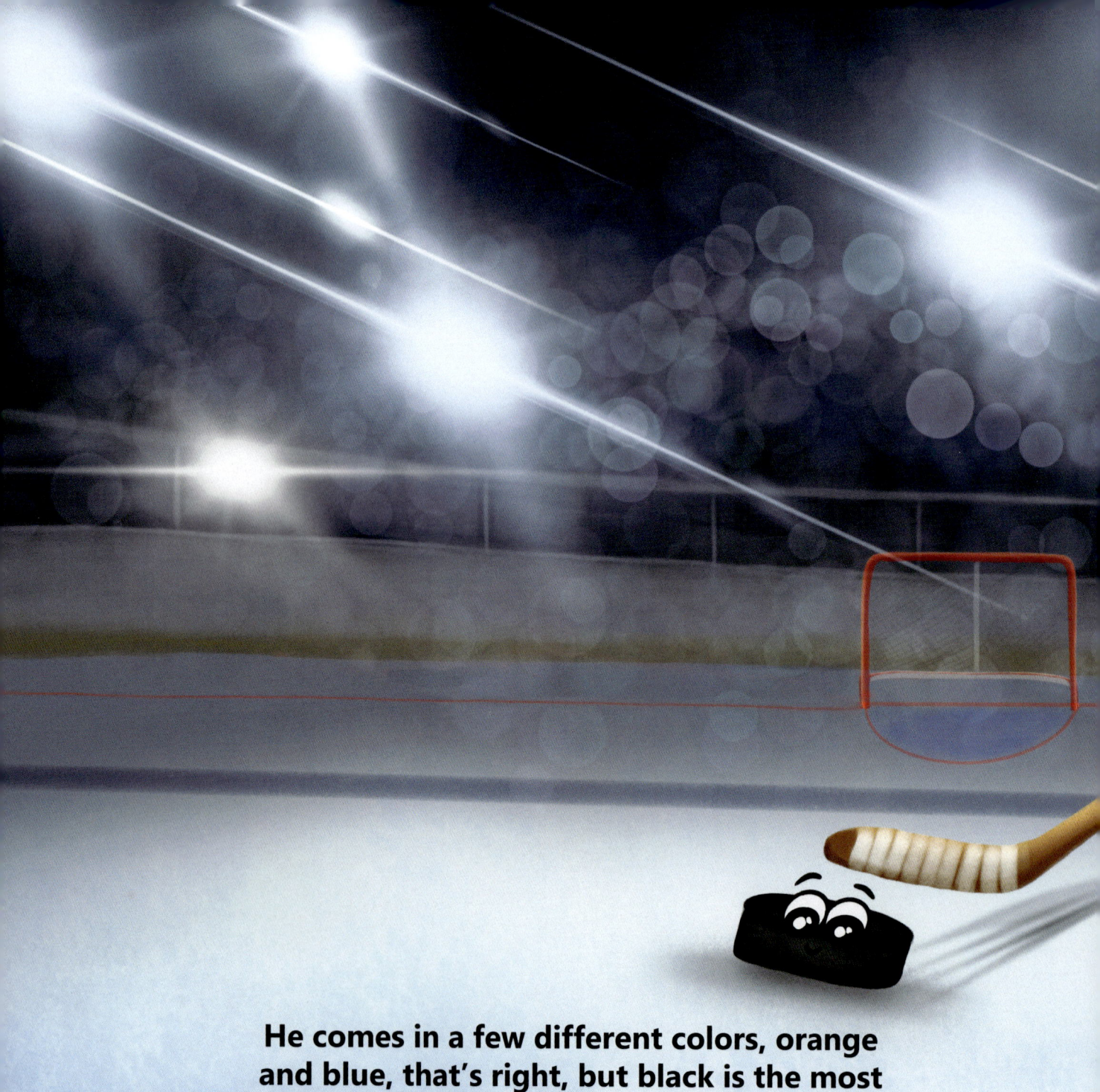

He comes in a few different colors, orange and blue, that's right, but black is the most common color you will see under the bright arena lights.

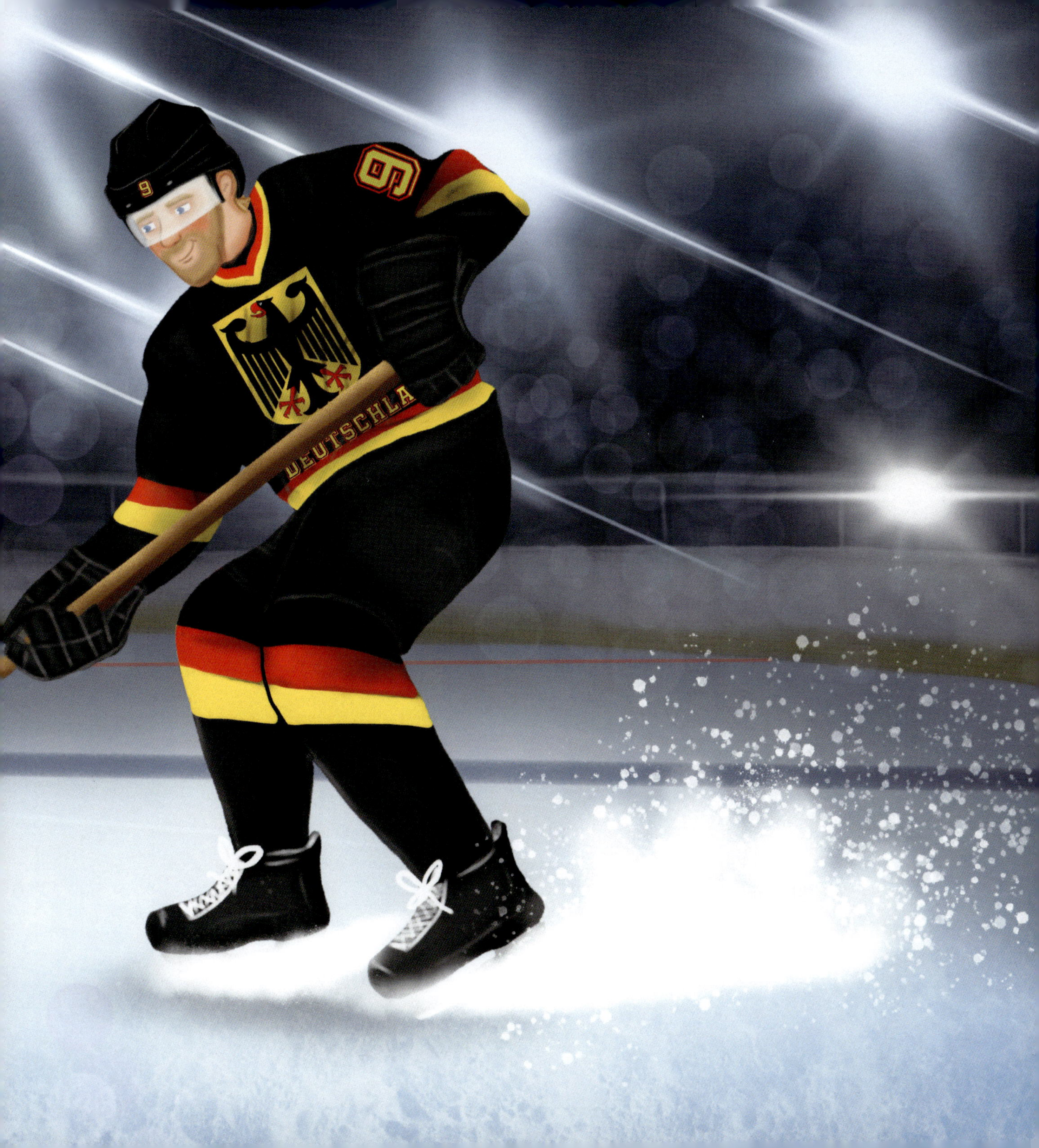
9
9
DEUTSCHLA

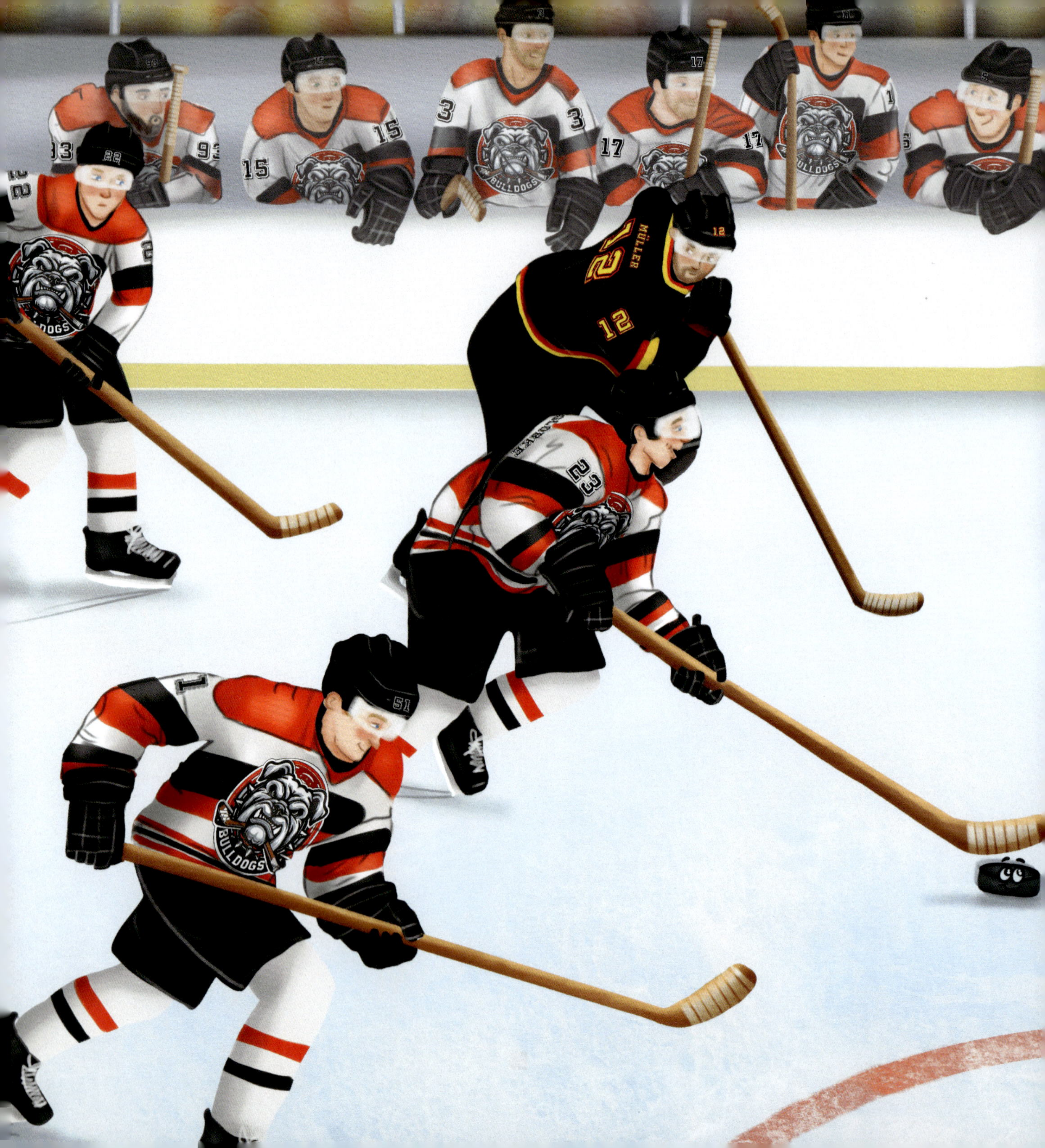
MÜLLER
12
BULLDOGS

Tuck loves creating the game of hockey, ensuring fun for everyone. He's the center of the game even though he doesn't weigh a ton.

When you hear the goal horn

BRRRRR!

He shoots, He scores!

THUMP!

TINK!

or

CLANG!

just know Tuck is nearby and never leaves without a

BANG!

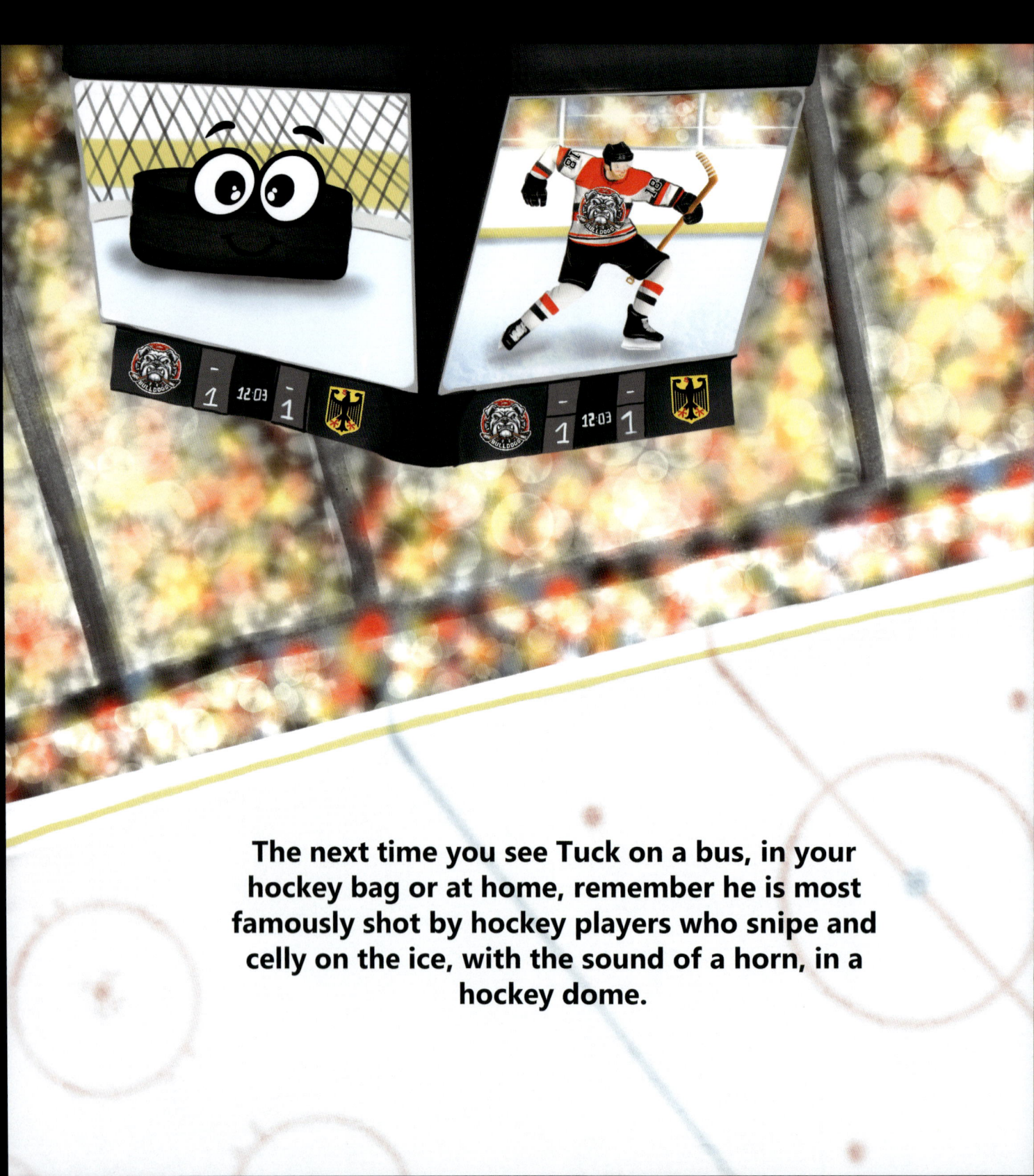

The next time you see Tuck on a bus, in your hockey bag or at home, remember he is most famously shot by hockey players who snipe and celly on the ice, with the sound of a horn, in a hockey dome.

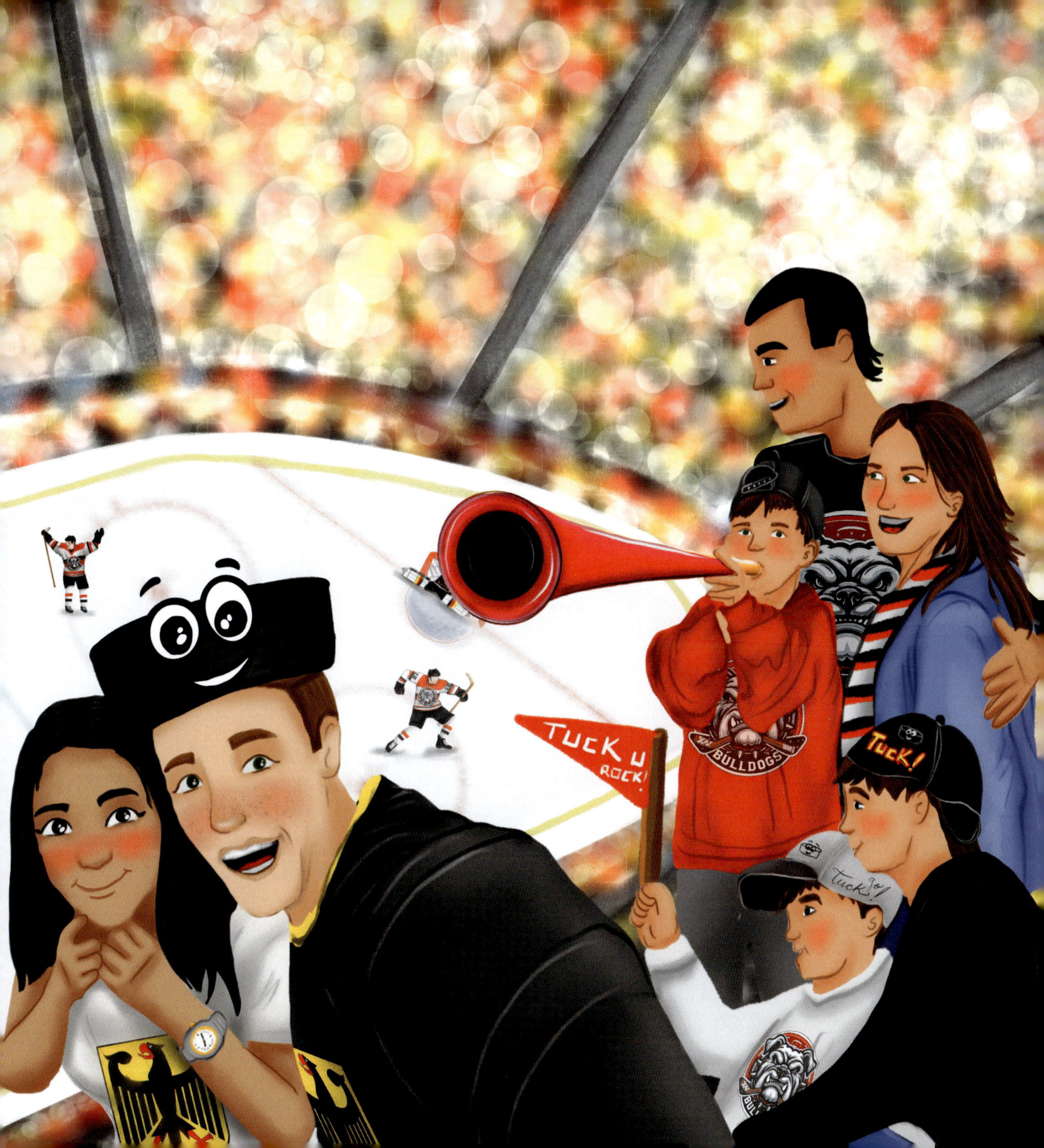
TUCK U
ROCK!
BULLDOGS
TUCK!

Meet the Author

Raised in rural Canadian town of Killaloe, Ontario, with a population of 700 people, Kaylie Globke began playing hockey at age seven leading to a lifelong passion for the sport. Skating on outdoor rinks and joining teams, often as the only girl until age 14, she saw the game evolve sparking her competitive drive. Since age 15, she has played for the German Black Eagles in her local community hockey tournament, Opeongo Heritage Cup. Years later, she accepted an offer to play for Carleton University's women's varsity hockey team while obtaining a bachelor's degree in communications. In her fourth year, she joined Athletes in Action, a Christian organization led by a couple who shared the good news of Jesus. Globke accepted Jesus Christ as her Lord and Savior, making a life-changing impact through the game she loves most. After graduation, she went on to play hockey overseas in the Swedish Women's Hockey League (SDHL) Division 1 for one year. Shortly after her return, she accepted an offer to work on one of North America's largest infrastructure projects, the Gordie Howe International Bridge with the Communications and Stakeholder Relations teams. During this time, she met her husband, Al, while the two volunteered with Hockey Ministries International volunteered at Adrian College, home of the Bulldogs. Both Globke's personal and professional passions have launched her into this next chapter as a children's picture book author. She resides in Michigan with her husband, two sons and dog, with aspirations to have more children in their hockey line-up. She currently plays in the top division of the Michigan Senior Women's Hockey League for the Bulldogs. The teams in *Tuck the Puck* highlight Globke's journey between two nations that hold special meaning in her life. Her family, hometown roots and team inspired *Tuck the Puck*.

Acknowledgements

I would first like to acknowledge my Lord and Savior, Jesus Christ. My life has been forever changed by what He did for a sinner like me on a cross all those years ago. I am forever grateful He met me through hockey and hope you are encouraged that He can change your life too. Romans 10:9 says, "Because, if you confess with your mouth that Jesus is Lord and believe in your heart that God raised him from the dead, you will be saved." This means free from the penalty of sin that He paid the price for. There is hope. If you have questions or would like to know more, please email The River Church at info@theriverchurch.cc. I would like to thank my husband, Al, for your unwavering support. You are my best friend and have always cheered me on. You are one of the best treasures that hockey gave me. I love you forever and always. To my children, you inspire me daily. Being your mom has been one of the greatest gifts in my life. I can't wait to watch you grow and at the same time, hope it slows down. I love you forever and always. Dad and mom, thank you. Without your financial investment, car rides and believing in me, I wouldn't have played hockey or written this book. I appreciate what you have done for me. I would like to recognize the Opeongo Heritage Cup organizers, coaching staff, my teammates, volunteers and sponsors. This tournament has played a significant role in my hockey journey. I am excited to highlight the German Black Eagles in *Tuck the Puck*. To my family, friends, teammates and colleagues, I am overwhelmed by your encouragement and assistance throughout this process. From the bottom of my heart, thank you. I would like to recognize authors, Andy Coats and Cara Brzezicki. Your wealth of knowledge is one of the reasons this book has been published. I am beyond thankful for your guidance. To my illustrator, Valeshka Escalona. Your tireless working around the clock and on weekend efforts are the backbone of this story. There aren't enough words to express my gratitude to you and your family. Thank you for your creativity, work ethic and friendship. I must also acknowledge that you are awesome for loving *Lord of the Rings* as much as I do. Check out her portfolio on Instagram at @valeshkart. To my readers, thank you for purchasing my book and supporting me in this journey. You believe in what we have created. I appreciate you so much. Thank you!